WELCOME TO
PASSPORT TO READING
A beginning reader's ticket to a brand-new world!

Every book in this program is designed to build read-along and read-alone skills, level by level, through engaging and enriching stories. As the reader turns each page, he or she will become more confident with new vocabulary, sight words, and comprehension.

These PASSPORT TO READING levels will help you choose the perfect book for every reader.

READING TOGETHER
Read short words in simple sentence structures together to begin a reader's journey.

READING OUT LOUD
Encourage developing readers to sound out words in more complex stories with simple vocabulary.

READING INDEPENDENTLY
Newly independent readers gain confidence reading more complex sentences with higher word counts.

READY TO READ MORE
Readers prepare for chapter books with fewer illustrations and longer paragraphs.

This book features sight words from the educator-supported Dolch Sight Word List. Readers will become more familiar with these commonly used vocabulary words, increasing reading speed and fluency.

For more information, please visit www.passporttoreadingbooks.com, where each reader can add stamps to a personalized passport while traveling through story after story!

Enjoy the journey!

Little, Brown and Company

Hachette Book Group
237 Park Avenue, New York, NY 10017
Visit our website at www.lb-kids.com

Little, Brown and Company is a division of Hachette Book Group, Inc.
The Little, Brown name and logo are trademarks of Hachette Book Group, Inc.

The publisher is not responsible for websites (or their content) that are not owned by the publisher.

First Edition: November 2011

ISBN 978-0-316-18577-6

10 9 8 7 6 5 4 3 2 1

CW

Printed in the United States of America

THE ADVENTURES OF ★
TINTIN
DANGER AT SEA

Adapted by Kirsten Mayer

Screenplay by Steven Moffat

and Edgar Wright & Joe Cornish

ased on The Adventures of Tintin series by Hergé

Little, Brown and Company
New York ★ Boston

Attention, Tintin fans!
Can you find these items in this book?

SEAPLANE

MANUAL

PROPELLER

SAND DUNE

Tintin and his dog, Snowy,
like to find clues and solve crimes.
Sometimes they get into trouble
while trying to solve a mystery.

Tintin is on the trail of missing treasure!
So is Captain Haddock.
Tintin and the captain work together
to escape the bad guys.

Tintin, Snowy, and their new friend
have found more trouble!
They are in a small lifeboat
in the middle of the wide-open sea!

"We must go to the city of Bagghar," says Tintin.

"There we will find a clue to the treasure. Can you get us there, Captain?"

"Give me those oars," says Haddock.
"I am master and commander of the seas!"

Haddock stands in the boat
to grab the oars from Tintin.
When he swings around,
the oars hit Tintin and Snowy!
He does not know
that he has knocked them out!

Haddock turns again.

"Look at the pair of them, fast asleep!

Never mind. I will get you there, Tintin."

The captain rows the boat for hours.

When Tintin wakes up,
he sees a fire inside the boat!
"Captain?" he asks. "What have you done?"

"You looked cold, so I lit a wee fire,"
explains Haddock.
"In a wooden boat?" cries Tintin.
Suddenly, the flames explode!

The three of them end up sitting
on top of the overturned boat.
"Well, this is a fine mess," says Tintin.
"Hopeless," agrees Haddock.

Snowy barks.

"What is it, Snowy?" asks Tintin.

He looks up. There is a seaplane!

Captain Haddock waves his arms.
"We are saved! We are saved!" he yells.
The plane banks toward the boat
and then begins to fire at them!
They are under attack!

"Captain, get down!" shouts Tintin.
Haddock jumps into the water
to hide behind the boat.

Tintin had saved a flare gun
from the lifeboat.
He fires the signal light,
and it hits the plane's engine.
"Well done, my boy!" cheers Haddock.

The seaplane's engine sputters out,
and the plane lands on the water.
They see two pilots climb out
and start fixing the engine.

"Wait here," says Tintin.

He swims over to the plane.

"Put your hands in the air!"

Tintin calls to the pilots in a bluff.

With the element of surprise,

Tintin and Haddock take care of the pilots.

But who will fly the plane?

Tintin looks through the manual.

"You do know what you are doing, right?"
asks Haddock.

"More or less," answers Tintin.

"Well, which is it? More or less?"

Tintin gets the plane in the air.

"We are off to Bagghar!" he says.

Haddock is still worried.

"Is there another way," he asks,

"that does not take us into that storm?"

There are big black clouds ahead.

Snowy barks. They fly right into them!

Lightning flashes.

"The fuel tank is almost empty," says Tintin.
"Captain, climb out of the plane
and pour fuel into the tank!"
"Christopher Columbus!" cries Haddock.
"There is a storm out there!"

"We are running on fumes!" yells Tintin.
Captain Haddock goes out the door
and manages to pour fuel into the tank.
The plane propeller spins again.
"Captain, it is working!" cries Tintin.

But Haddock sees something.

"Land! Land!" he shouts.

"We are not there yet," replies Tintin.

Then he sees it, too: a huge sand dune!

Tintin manages to miss the dune,
but there are more ahead.
They are going to crash!
"Hang on!" cries Haddock.
The plane smashes into the sand,
but they are okay!

The three friends set off across the sand on their next adventure.

"We have to keep going!" says Tintin.

"On to Bagghar and to the treasure!"